ISABELLE DE CHARRIERE

Letters of Mistress Henley
Published by Her Friend

Texts and Translations
Modern Language Association of America

Carmen Chaves Tesser, chair; Eugene C. Eoyang, Michael R. Katz, Robert J. Rodini, Judith L. Ryan, Mario J. Valdés, and Renée Waldinger, series editors

Texts

1. Isabelle de Charrière, *Lettres de Mistriss Henley publiées par son amie.* Ed. Joan Hinde Stewart and Philip Stewart. 1993.
2. Françoise de Graffigny, *Lettres d'une Péruvienne.* Introd. Joan DeJean and Nancy K. Miller. 1993.

Translations

1. Isabelle de Charrière, *Letters of Mistress Henley Published by Her Friend.* Trans. Philip Stewart and Jean Vaché. 1993.
2. Françoise de Graffigny, *Letters from a Peruvian Woman.* Trans. David Kornacker. 1993.

ISABELLE DE CHARRIERE

Letters of Mistress Henley Published by Her Friend

Translated by
Philip Stewart and Jean Vaché

Introduction, Notes, and Bibliography
by Joan Hinde Stewart
and Philip Stewart

August 1997

The Modern Language Association of America
New York   1993

Library of Congress Cataloging-in-Publication Data

Charrière, Isabelle de, 1740–1805.
    [Lettres de Mistriss Henley publiées par son amie. English]
    Letters of Mistress Henley published by her friend / Isabelle
de Charrière ; translated by Philip Stewart and Jean Vaché ; introduction, notes, and bibliography by Joan Hinde Stewart and
Philip Stewart.
      p.   cm. — (Texts and translations. Translations ; 1)
    Includes bibliographical references.
    ISBN 0-87352-776-3 (paper)
    1. England—Social life and customs—18th century—Fiction.
2. Married women—England—Fiction. 3. Marriage—England—
Fiction. I. Stewart, Joan Hinde. II. Stewart, Philip. III. Title.
IV. Series.
PQ1963.C55L4813   1993
843' .5—dc20   93-26862

Published by The Modern Language Association of America
10 Astor Place, New York, New York 10003-6981

Printed on recycled paper

TABLE OF CONTENTS

ACKNOWLEDGMENTS

The authoritative edition of *Lettres de Mistriss Henley publiées par son amie,* edited by Dennis M. Wood, with an introduction by Christabel Braunrot and notes by Christabel Braunrot and Maurice Gilot, is in volume 8 of the van Oorschot edition of the *Œuvres complètes* (see bibliography). The kind permission of the publishers to use that text in preparing this translation is gratefully acknowledged. We are also grateful to the College of Humanities and Social Sciences at North Carolina State University for a research award that supported the preparation of the present edition; to Janet Altman, James Rolleston, and English Showalter for comments; and to Susan Marston for editorial suggestions.

INTRODUCTION

In *Letters of Mistress Henley Published by Her Friend* (*Lettres de Mistriss Henley publiées par son amie*), an explicitly literary provocation is fused with distinctly autobiographical elements to produce a text—"occasional" in the fullest sense—that we are only now learning to read on its own terms. Its original publication was greeted with enthusiasm and controversy, and then for years it was more or less ignored. Recently scholars have begun to acknowledge it as probably the most brilliant short novel of one of the most original writers of the French eighteenth century—a woman who wasn't even French.

It is, in the first place, as its opening lines make clear, a feminist response to another novel—indeed, another remarkable Swiss novel: *Le mari sentimental* ("The Sentimental Husband"), which appeared anonymously in fall 1783 but was soon known to be the work of Samuel de Constant. His hero is a country gentleman and retired military man of forty-six, M. de Bompré, who writes a series of seventeen letters to M. de Saint-Thomin, a friend whose wedding Bompré has just attended. Saint-Thomin's marital happiness makes Bompré, who has just lost his father, feel dissatisfied with his bachelor life among the peasants and hunters, his old servants, and his faithful dog and horse, and he begins to think seriously about getting married himself. In Geneva he meets an eligible woman of thirty-five, sister-in-law of a retired officer with whom he once served. She strikes Bompré as charming and witty, if a trifle pretentious and intolerant, and within four days he agrees to wed her. "Happiness awaited me at forty-six; I never would have thought it," he writes in a lyrical announcement of his engagement (71, 1975 edition; our trans.).

But when Bompré returns with his new wife to the country, a series of events, at first apparently trivial and then more and more desolating, reveals that she has no heart. She practices emotional blackmail on her husband and sets about assiduously trying to turn his rustic home into an elegant residence, removing the portrait of his father from the dining room; adding expensive wallpapers, alcoves, and wood paneling; and entertaining her fancy and insolent friends. In her spare time, she closes herself in and reads novels. Bompré wants to be adaptable, conceding "in different times, different customs" (89), and trying to foster the kind of bond he admired in his friend's marriage. But with self-assured egotism, his wife rejects each of his attempts at communication. "My dear friend," he confides to his correspondent, "I understand nothing about marriage; I am constantly in the wrong, and none of my ideas are realized" (93). When, with a cruel kind of coldness and indifference to him, she has his dog, Hector, shot, maneuvers his loyal servants into leaving, requires that the sturdy horse who once saved his life be replaced with a pair of carriage horses, and even accuses him of seducing a young peasant,

Bompré decides to kill himself. He sends his friend a suicide letter to express the "horror, indignation, and despair" (182) that overwhelm him. In a terse afterword, we learn that the widow remarries and that her new husband makes her happy.

Isabelle de Charrière found the city of Geneva absorbed with *Le mari sentimental* when she traveled there, in early 1784, to arrange for the printing of her *Lettres neuchâteloises* ("Letters from Neuchâtel"). In a day when novels were still often taken "for real," the public was so inclined to credit the "truth" of this misogynist story that at least one poor woman, a widow named Mme Caillat, whose husband had committed suicide after a year of marriage, felt compelled to attest in a notarized document that she had treated him with affection and was therefore not the novel's model. Constant corroborated her testimony, but no one—as Charrière added, in recounting the event years later—believed him (letter to Baron Taets van Amerongen, Jan. 1804 [*Œuvres complètes* 6: 559]; see also Godet, *Madame de Charrière* 263).

A somewhat sententious M. de Bompré, while still a bachelor, writes:

> I have often heard arguments about what is most important in a marriage; to some it is beauty, to others fortune, or wit, or a gentle character: I have always thought it should be reason; reason reduces everything to truth, it is the delight of the moment and is found everywhere and in everything. With reason, good increases and evil diminishes.
>
> (73)

Charrière was moved by this encomium to uncover a darker side of reason. *Letters of Mistress Henley,* her competing version of the unhappy marriage of a country gentleman, appeared anonymously just a few months later. Her novel is rigorously parallel to Constant's in its epistolary form (the most popular fictional form of the time) and in theme. Analogous elements include the boredom of country life, the dog, and the portrait, as well as the act of reading a novel—*Le mari sentimental* itself—with which Charrière's story begins. But each such element carries a subtly but crucially different meaning, a new naturalness and poignancy, and the letters of Charrière's heroine, without verbiage or sententiousness, are patterned and nuanced to convey an entirely different sense from that of Constant's novel. Mistress Henley's account of a woman who cannot make a place for herself in the life of a middle-aged man whose habits, alliances, and surroundings are comfortably established—a woman who, despite her best efforts, is always, inevitably, wrong—becomes cautionary: "Many women are in the same situation as I."

If, moreover, the wife in Constant's tale is in no way admirable, the husband in Charrière's is, if not "perfect," at least a model of consistency and probity, and Charrière's originality has to do with creating a story of desperate unhappiness in which there are no villains and all the causes are internal. Here is a woman who is free to choose her own companion and who selects a decent, affectionate, and estimable man, a good husband, father, and master, only to discover that she cannot bear sharing his life. The novel has an exceptional density, both because of Charrière's plain but powerful and often ironic formulations—the turns she gives to familiar words and expres-

wet nurse?

sions—and because decisions like whether or not to nurse the baby become so highly charged. There are, moreover, numerous internal contrasts and parallels: for example, the fact that Lord B. stands for election and Mr. Henley declines to do so; the comparable unsuitability of Mistress Henley and her maid, Fanny, for country life; the problems of dress and ornamentation for Mistress Henley and her stepdaughter; the allusions to the Indies (where the "nabob," Lord Bridgewater, made his fortune and the peasant father in the same hope wants to send his son); the recurring tension between old and new (furniture, generations, wives).

The unhappiness, even despair, generated by all the novel's "rational" choices seems to have been unusually threatening to some early readers. For although Mistress Henley comments only on her own immediate condition, her words indict a whole social and economic system, one that makes it difficult for an unmarried woman to subsist and all but impossible for a sensitive woman to endure married life. A contemporary, Pastor Chaillet, adopting Mistress Henley's own words in her first letter, called the novel an "appealing, cruel little book, literarily excellent, but in my opinion morally dangerous in various ways" (Charrière, *Œuvres complètes* 2: 420). But the success of so morally dubious a story was, by Charrière's account, impressive. *Letters of Mistress Henley*, she wrote twenty years later, caused a "schism" in the society of Geneva:

> All the husbands were for Mr. Henley; many wives were for Mrs. Henley; and the girls didn't dare say what they thought. Never did fictional characters seem so real, and people asked me for clarifications, as though I had known

identifying w/ characters

them other than on paper. I have heard very polite people
trade insults about this. I was sometimes embarrassed.

(letter to Baron Taets van Amerongen,
Jan. 1804 [*Œuvres complètes* 6: 559])

Charrière's embarrassment must have had more than
a little to do with the fact that she and her husband were
considered the originals of her protagonists (editor's pref-
ace to *Lettres de Mistriss Henley, Œuvres complètes* 8: 96). In
her mid-forties at the time of publication, Charrière was
a resident of Le Pontet, her husband's property near the
Swiss village of Colombier, near Neuchâtel; but she was
known throughout Europe as a formidable intellectual.
Until her marriage, she had been called Belle de Zuylen,
for she was born to one of the first families of Holland
and christened Isabella Agneta Elisabeth van Tuyll van
Serooskerken van Zuylen. Her birth consigned her to a
society that was rigid, class-conscious, and occasionally
suffocating but that instilled in her a deep loyalty to family
and gave her the means to read widely in the French clas-
sics and learn the impeccable French in which she wrote
almost exclusively. (No less an authority than Sainte-
Beuve would describe her writing as "the very best French,
the French of Versailles" [444].)

But she began early to dream of escape, and through
literature—fiction, essays, plays, letters—she did indeed
forge an identity, both in the eyes of her contemporaries
and for posterity, that was different from that of a provin-
cial Dutch aristocrat. Her major novels would not appear
until the 1780s and 1790s. Along with *Lettres de Mistriss
Henley publiées par son amie* (1784), they include *Lettres neuchâteloises* (1784), *Lettres écrites de Lausanne* (1785; "Letters

Written from Lausanne"), *Caliste ou continuation des* Lettres écrites de Lausanne (1787; "Caliste; or, Continuation of *Letters Written from Lausanne*"), *Trois femmes* (1796; "Three Women"), *Honorine d'Userche* (1798), and *Sainte-Anne* (1799). But in her early twenties she had already published her first short novel, *Le noble* (1763; "The Nobleman"), a whimsical and iconoclastic tale about the silliness of the pretensions of nobility. It scandalized friends and relatives and did not make it easier for her to find in marriage an escape from the constraints of life in her parents' home.

Indeed, when we read the story of the problematic marriageability of the protagonist whom we know only as "S. Henley"—she needs to marry for social and economic security, but, discerning and disabused, she turns down offers and thus becomes the uneasy object of criticism—we are reminded that Belle de Zuylen's own highly visible drama was the finding of a husband. Suitors trooped past, both domestic and foreign (the most famous was James Boswell), but they were too common, too Catholic, too poor, too profligate, or, finally, too awed by her. In her correspondence, which fills six dense volumes of her complete works, the most gripping of the letters from this period are those detailing her negotiations with a motley crew of potential husbands and the father whom she tried to manipulate.

When she was twenty years old, her path crossed that of another member of the talented and idiosyncratic Constant clan centered in Geneva and Lausanne. At a ball in The Hague she met Baron Louis David Constant d'Hermenches (oldest brother of Samuel), a Swiss officer in the Dutch service. Eighteen years older than she, he was a husband, a father, and a rake; but instead of an affair they began a correspondence, secret at first, that lasted for many years. It reveals her as sensual, frank, lucid, and logical, an independent thinker and a true citizen of the European Enlightenment. (Her letters to d'Hermenches are matched in interest only by those she passionately wrote years later to his eccentric nephew, Benjamin Constant, whom she met in Paris in 1787.) With d'Hermenches she discussed her marriage prospects in particular, and he, despite his love for her, proposed a union with another officer, his friend the Marquis de Bellegarde; but Bellegarde's Catholicism and his debts, among other things, got in the way, and like her other prospects, this one fell through.

She finally succeeded only at the age of thirty, when she persuaded her father to allow her to accept an offer from her brothers' former tutor, an orderly Swiss gentleman, Charles-Emmanuel de Charrière de Penthaz. The wedding left him sick from punch and her with a raging toothache. After a honeymoon trip to Paris, they settled in a quiet Swiss village with the groom's father and two unmarried sisters, one of whom gardened while the other ran the household with an iron hand. There Isabelle de Charrière was to live for thirty-five years, until her death in 1805. She would have liked to have children.

But if something like the accidental confluence of the publication of *Le mari sentimental* and Isabelle de Charrière's own marital situation as wife to a good and stolid man inspired the writing of this novel, it must also be stressed that these events are transmuted into a sort of allegory of the contemporary novelistic vision. In scope and significance, Charrière's work has been compared with the epistolary novels of two of the best and most popular writers of the second half of the eighteenth century, Marie Jeanne Riccoboni and Jean-Jacques Rousseau: with Riccoboni's fiction for its meditation on women's fate and with Rousseau's *Julie ou la nouvelle Héloïse* (1761) for its portrayal of married life. One needs to remember that plots of novels had long been characterized by the antics of passionate lovers and by all manner of adventure and coincidence: shipwrecks, disguises, illicit or secret marriages, disputed legacies, lost or stolen letters, seductions and assaults. Charrière, like Constant, Rousseau, and Riccoboni at her best, tends to eschew such commonplaces. Moreover, in the way in which she anatomizes the apparently trivial, the intensely domestic, the unsayable and almost the unthinkable, she goes beyond her precursors, making *Letters of Mistress Henley* not only one of the most moving but also one of the most modern works of its day. Whereas Bompré, in his seventeen long letters, is inclined to digress at length on politics and agricultural economy, Mistress Henley, who resorts neither to rhetorical flourishes nor to flights into abstraction, never diverges from her immediate concern, which is the amorphous pain and frustration of a feeling woman in the house of an all too reasonable man.

And if *Le mari sentimental* is also devoid of forced marriages and lost wills, nevertheless the putative adultery, the grandiloquence of the suicide letter, and especially the suicide itself all link it to a certain tradition of romantic adventures, where infidelity was a standard component and acceptable conclusions to novels were largely limited to marriage or death. In Charrière's novel, by contrast, there is no question of infidelity and there is no concluding suicide. Here and elsewhere in a body of writing where very little seems to "happen" in recognizable fictional terms, we have a disconcertingly open ending: the last line leaves unresolved the question of the heroine's happiness, indeed the very question of her survival, posing only the alternative death or some more "reasonable" resolution. The beginning anticipates the end, insofar as the epigraph is uncertainly suspended like the story itself. And the epigraph is, needless to say, an oblique commentary on that uncertain situation: a line from a fable by La Fontaine that turns up years earlier in Charrière's correspondence. In 1768, discouraged in her lengthy negotiations with Bellegarde, she wrote to d'Hermenches, "'I've seen many marriages, none of them tempts me,' says La Fontaine and I say so too" (*Œuvres complètes* 2: 73).

The year after the original 1784 Geneva publication of the novel, an unauthorized Paris edition, blurring questions of authorship, put the Constant and the Charrière novels together with a third piece called *La justification de M. Henley* ("The Justification of Mr. Henley"). This last, a pedestrian and overblown attempt at a sequel, takes the story to its "logical" and banal conclusion by incorporating into a bathetic account of Mr. Henley's conduct and regrets an announcement of Mistress Henley's death in childbirth. The extent of Charrière's originality in defying established norms for endings can be gauged if one considers the reviews this volume received in two of the most established periodicals, *L'année littéraire* and the *Mercure de France*. While both comment on the paucity of action, the absence of passion, and the remarkable challenge of rendering a marriage interesting, both strikingly misread

Charrière's conclusion. Inadvertently—perhaps inevitably—conflating *Letters of Mistress Henley* with *La justification* (although the *Mercure* categorically declared the *Justification* so inferior that it could not be by the same hand as Mistress Henley's letters), both commentators allude to Mistress Henley's "death" and criticize its excessive pathos: "she dies in childbirth. This is really taking things a bit too tragically," writes the *Mercure* (191). *L'année littéraire* is yet more explicit: "One might believe and rightly so . . . that what the author recounts is hardly sufficient to make one die of sorrow. Whatever one's sensibility, this is carrying it much too far" (179–80). While the reviewers condescendingly read a woman's domestic chagrin as incompatible with despair, they are virtually blind to Charrière's unconventional gesture of leaving the fate of her heroine an open question, so that they pass right through it and on to Mistress Henley's presumed demise.

The subtlety of the text and its refusal to conclude in a codifiable manner have given rise to numerous interpretations. To Sainte-Beuve, Mistress Henley is the consummate "misunderstood" woman (443), whereas for Robert Mauzi, writing in 1960, the woman misunderstood is a role she only "plays at" (479). More remarkably, critics have taken her compulsive self-criticism at face value: for Mauzi she is testy and juvenile; for Sigyn Minier-Birk she is vain and proud, her frivolous behavior poisoning her conjugal relations. Germaine de Staël (who incidentally became Charrière's rival for the affections of Benjamin Constant) complained of Charrière's annoying habit of getting readers hooked and then failing to finish the story. One of Charrière's best recent critics, however, Susan Jackson, explains this refusal to conclude as performing, like all the unfinished needlework in Charrière's stories, an "important illustrative function": for Charrière, female life, like female *ouvrage*, is "open-ended, subject to change for better or worse, perhaps tedious, even trivial, but at least not necessarily or uniformly tragic" ("Novels" 301, 303). Indeed, for a feminist reader of the late twentieth century, the "unfinished" *Letters of Mistress Henley* indirectly expresses the way all fictional endings are driven by the needs of patriarchy and tend to entail the obliteration of female perspectives.

Catering to epistolary form and the English setting so much in vogue, responding to a novel by her compatriot and perhaps also to Rousseau's wildly popular *Julie*, even while taking inspiration from her own rather depressing experience as a marriageable and then a married woman of culture, sensibility, and means, Charrière gives unexpected shape and texture to a story of a woman's life in a modern (that is, consensual) marriage. Without the usual tyrannical parents of novels, the match is no more arranged than it is the inevitable product of passion: it is a marriage of reason. And therein lies the paradox, and the menace. When the heroine has to settle on her own husband, her dilemma is resolved, through the imperatives of her female conditioning, in favor of neither glamour nor gold but of the least "vulgar" decision. The background against which her marriage evolves is domestic and conjugal life in its most private and quotidian— and agonizingly empty—form. The touching figure who emerges from this story is one of the most compelling and saddest representations of European womanhood in the late eighteenth century.

PRINCIPAL WORKS OF
Isabelle de Charrière

Le noble, 1763
Portrait de Zélide, 1763
Lettres neuchâteloises, 1784
Lettres de Mistriss Henley publiées par son amie, 1784 ✳
Lettres écrites de Lausanne, 1785
Caliste ou continuation des Lettres écrites de Lausanne, 1787
Observations et conjectures politiques, 1787–88
Plainte et défense de Thérèse Levasseur, 1789
Eloge de Jean-Jacques Rousseau, 1790
Aiglonette et Insinuante ou la souplesse, 1791
Lettres trouvées dans la neige, 1793
Lettres trouvées dans des portefeuilles d'émigrés, 1793
L'émigré, 1793
Trois femmes, 1796
Honorine d'Userche, 1798
Sainte-Anne, 1799
Les ruines de Yedburg, 1799
Sir Walter Finch et son fils William, 1806

BIBLIOGRAPHY

Complete Works of Isabelle de Charrière

Œuvres complètes. Ed. Jean-Daniel Candaux, C. P. Courtney, Pierre H. Dubois, Simone Dubois-De Bruyn, Patrice Thompson, Jeroom Vercruysse, and Dennis M. Wood. 10 vols. Amsterdam: van Oorschot, 1979–84.

Principal Editions of *Lettres de Mistriss Henley publiées par son amie* (in Chronological Order)

Lettres de Mistriss Henley, publiées par son amie. Geneva, 1784.

Le mari sentimental, ou le mariage comme il y en a quelques-uns, *suivi des* Lettres de Mistriss Henley, publiées par son amie, Mde de C*** de Z***, *et de la* Justification de M. Henley, adressée à l'amie de sa femme. Geneva and Paris: Buisson, 1785.

Lettres neuchâteloises. Mistriss Henley. Le noble. Ed. Philippe Godet. Geneva: Jullien, 1908.

Constant, Samuel de. Le mari sentimental, *suivi des* Lettres de Mrs Henley *de Mme de Charrière.* Ed. Pierre Kohler. Geneva: Lettres de Lausanne, 1928.

Belle de Zuylen. *Mistriss Henley.* Paris: Mangart, 1944. (Published clandestinely by Stols, The Hague, during the German occupation of Holland [see Courtney, *Preliminary Bibliography*].)

Belle van Zuylen. *Mistriss Henley*. Burins de Michel Béret. Utrecht: Société "De Roos," 1952.

Lettres de Mistriss Henley publiées par son amie. Ed. Dennis M. Wood, with introd. by Christabel Braunrot and notes by Braunrot and Maurice Gilot. Amsterdam: van Oorschot, 1980. Vol. 8 of *Œuvres complètes*.

Romans: Lettres écrites de Lausanne, Trois femmes, Lettres de Mistriss Henley, Lettres neuchâteloises. Paris: Chemin Vert, 1982.

English Translation

Four Tales by Zélide. Trans. S[ybil] M[arjorie] S[cott]. (Includes *The Nobleman, Mistress Henley, Letters from Lausanne,* and *Letters from Lausanne–Caliste*.) London: Constable, 1925; New York: Scribner's, 1926. Reissued as *Four Tales*. Freeport: Books for Libraries, 1970.

Other Modern Editions of Novels by Isabelle de Charrière

Caliste ou Lettres écrites de Lausanne. Ed. Claudine Hermann. Paris: Des Femmes, 1979.

Honorine d'Userche. Toulouse: Ombres, 1992.

Lettres écrites de Lausanne. (Includes Rousseau's *Julie ou la nouvelle Héloïse*.) Ed. Jean Starobinski. Lausanne: Rencontre, 1970.

Lettres neuchâteloises. Ed. Isabelle Vissière and Jean-Louis Vissière. Pref. by Christophe Calame. Paris: Différence, 1991.

Lettres neuchâteloises *suivi de* Trois femmes. Ed. Charly Guyot. Lausanne: Bibliothèque Romande, 1971.

Modern Edition of *Le mari sentimental*

Constant, Samuel de. *Le mari sentimental ou le mariage comme il y en a quelques-uns*. Ed. Giovanni Riccioli. Milan: Cisalpino-Goliardica, 1975.

Eighteenth-Century Reviews
of *Lettres de Mistriss Henley*

L'année littéraire 1785 8: 169–80.

Journal de Paris 13 May 1786: 537–38.

Mercure de France 22 Apr. 1786: 186–93. Rpt. in *Mercure de France*. Vol. 130. Geneva: Slatkine, 1974. 377–79.

Selected Criticism and Commentary
on Isabelle de Charrière

Bérenguier, Nadine. "From Clarens to Hollow Park, Isabelle de Charrière's Quiet Revolution." *Studies in Eighteenth-Century Culture* 21 (1991): 219–43.

Courtney, C. P. "Isabelle de Charrière and the 'Character of H. B. Constant': A False Attribution." *French Studies* 36.3 (1982): 282–89.

Fink, Beatrice, ed. *Isabelle de Charrière/Belle Van Zuylen*. Spec. issue of *Eighteenth-Century Life* 13. ns 1 (1989): 1–78.

Godet, Philippe. *Madame de Charrière et ses amis*. Geneva: Jullien, 1906.

Jackson, Susan K. "Disengaging Isabelle: Professional Rhetoric and Female Friendship in the Correspondence of Mme de Charrière and Mlle de Gélieu." Fink 26–41.

———. "The Novels of Isabelle de Charrière; or, A Woman's Work Is Never Done." *Studies in Eighteenth-Century Culture* 14 (1985): 299–306.

Lacy, Margriet Bruyn. "Madame de Charrière and the Constant Family." *Romance Notes* 23.2 (1982): 154–58.

Lanser, Susan S. "Courting Death: *Roman, Romantisme*, and *Mistress Henley*'s Narrative Practices." Fink 49–59.

MacArthur, Elizabeth J. "Devious Narratives: Refusal of Closure in Two Eighteenth-Century Epistolary Novels." *Eighteenth-Century Studies* 21.1 (1987): 1–20.

Mauzi, Robert. "Les maladies de l'âme au XVIIIe siècle." *Revue des sciences humaines*, fasc. 100 (Oct.–Dec. 1960): 459–93.

Sainte-Beuve, C.-A. "Madame de Charrière." *Portraits de femmes*. Paris: Garnier, 1882. 411–57.

Scott, Geoffrey. *The Portrait of Zélide*. New York: Scribner's, 1927.

Stewart, Joan Hinde. "Designing Women." *A New History of French Literature*. Ed. Denis Hollier. Cambridge: Harvard UP, 1989. 553–58.

———. *Gynographs: French Novels by Women of the Late Eighteenth Century*. Lincoln: U of Nebraska P, 1993.

West, Anthony. *Mortal Wounds*. New York: McGraw, 1973.

Whatley, Janet. "Isabelle de Charrière." *French Women Writers: A Bio-bibliographical Source Book*. Ed. Eva Martin Sartori and Dorothy Wynne Zimmerman. New York: Greenwood, 1991. 35–46.

Charrière Bibliographies

Courtney, C. P. *A Preliminary Bibliography of Isabelle de Charrière (Belle de Zuylen)*. Studies on Voltaire and the Eighteenth Century 186. Oxford: Voltaire Foundation, 1980.

———. *Isabelle de Charrière (Belle de Zuylen): A Secondary Bibliography*. Oxford: Voltaire Foundation; Paris: Touzot, 1982.

NOTE ON THE TEXT

The text of *Lettres de Mistriss Henley publiées par son amie*
appearing in volume 8 of the *Œuvres complètes* has been
used as the basis for the present translation. The regular-
ized modern protocol for quotations not yet having
evolved, Isabelle de Charrière and her original editors
used several different typographical forms for quotations:
italics, double quotation marks, single quotation marks,
and dashes (also used for nonquotation purposes). Single
quotation marks, for example, often seem to indicate con-
jectural utterances, repeated utterances, or thoughts that
may or may not be uttered. But, on the whole, the variety
of usage signals not a real narrative strategy but rather a
genuine stylistic liberty and a largely oral relation to the
story, not to mention the possibly arbitrary interventions
of a typesetter. To make the text more readable for a modern audience, we have rendered all clear quotation strate-
gies by quotation marks, while leaving in place dashes
used for other purposes; we have also paragraphed all
direct discourse.

ISABELLE DE CHARRIERE

Letters of Mistress Henley
Published by Her Friend

I've seen many marriages, etc.[1]
—La Fontaine

First Letter

What an appealing and cruel little book we got from your country a few weeks ago! Why had you not mentioned it to me, my dear friend, in your last letter? It can't have failed to create a sensation there; it has just been translated, and I am sure that *The Sentimental Husband*[2] will be in everyone's hands. I had read it in French, and was tormented by it. These past few days I have read it in English to my husband. My dear friend, this book, apparently so instructive, will be the cause of much injustice: Bompré ladies will not recognize themselves in it, or will hardly worry their heads about it; and their husbands will drive themselves crazy trying to understand, as if it had never been written. Women who little resemble Mrs. Bompré and who yet are women will be tormented by it, and their husbands... In reading alone the story of the portrait, the furniture switched around, poor Hector,[3] I painfully remembered a portrait, a piece of furniture, a dog: but the portrait was not of my father-in-law, the dog is full of life, and my husband is hardly bothered about it; as for the furnishing of my room, it seemed to me that it

---

[1](Title page) Charrière truncates with an ironic *etc.* this line from La Fontaine's "Le mal marié": "J'ai vu beaucoup d'hymens; aucuns d'eux ne me tentent" 'I've seen many marriages; none of them tempts me' (*Fables*, bk. 7).

[2]*Le mari sentimental*, by Samuel de Constant (1783). See introduction.

[3]Hector the dog, like the servants Nanon and Antoine mentioned a few lines further down, all figure in Constant's novel.

should suit me, and not my grandmothers' taste. In reading all that to my husband, instead of his feeling such differences even more than I, as I had fondly imagined in undertaking the reading, or not at all feeling this sort of resemblance, I saw him sometimes smile, sometimes sigh; he muttered a few words, petted his dog, and looked up where the portrait used to be. My dear friend, they will all think of themselves as being like Mr. Bompré, and will be surprised at how patiently they have borne life. That man made a great mistake, after all, when he married. His happiness, his whole destiny was too well settled; there was nothing for his wife to do but share sensations that were new and strange to her; she had no Nanon, no Antoine, no Hector, no neighbors to oblige, no relations, no habits; there wasn't enough there to occupy an existence. I would forgive her her books, her novels, her boredom, were it not for her hardness of heart, the wrong thinking and the horrible ending that it all brings about. In truth, my dear friend, if I were to condemn her I think I would be pronouncing my own condemnation. I too am not happy, no more so than the Sentimental Husband, although I am not like him at all, nor is my husband anything like his wife; he is even, if not as tender, just as communicative, and at least as calm and kind as that excellent husband. Would you like, my dear friend, for me to give you the history of my marriage, of the time that led up to it, and describe my life as it is today?

I will tell you some things you already know, so that you may better understand, or rather to make it easier to tell you those you do not know. Shall I tell you the thought that occurs to me? If my letter or letters are near the mark and seem to you likely to arouse interest, even enough to get them read, then translate them, changing the names, and omitting whatever seems to you tedious or unnecessary. I think many women are in my situation. I should like, if not to correct, then at least to caution husbands; I should like to put everything in its proper place, and for each one to see himself as he is.[*] One slight scruple however does give me pause in my project, but it is indeed slight. I have no serious complaints to make: Mr. Henley will not be recognized; he will no doubt never read what I write; and what if he did read it, and recognize himself!... Let me begin.

An orphan and an almost penniless one at a tender age, I was raised like those who are wealthiest, and with a tenderness that a mother's love could not surpass. My aunt, Lady Alesford, having lost her only daughter, adopted me in her stead, and by dint of caring for me and looking after me, came to love me as if I had been her daughter. Her husband had a nephew who was to inherit his property and title: it was intended that I become his wife. He was amiable, we were the same age,

---

[*]Or, implicitly, *herself as she is*, since the French word (*chacun*) is not gender-specific.

we were raised in the expectation of being united. This idea pleased us both; we loved each other without anxiety. His uncle died. This change in his fortune did not alter his heart; but he was sent to travel. In Venice he would still have been Rousseau's Lord John; he would have torn up the marquise's cuffs:[5] but in Florence, more seductive charms caused me to fade from his mind. He spent some time in Naples, and the following year he died in Paris. I shall not attempt to tell you how I suffered then, all I had already suffered for several months. You saw in Montpellier[6] the traces that grief had left on my temper, and its effect on my health. My aunt was hardly less afflicted than I. Fifteen years of hope, fifteen years nourishing a favorite project, all had flown away, all was lost. As for me, I had lost all that a woman can lose. At twenty our hearts lead us to believe we may yet have resources, and I returned to England a little less unhappy than I had left it. My travels had formed and emboldened me; I could speak French more easily, and could sing better; I was admired. Men made overtures, and all it

---

[5]Allusion to an anecdote in book 5 of Rousseau's *Emile* that exemplifies a young man's fidelity to the girl he left at home. Lord John is a young Englishman whose governor has taken him on the grand tour. In Venice, a lady (Rousseau doesn't say she is a marquise) gives him a pair of cuffs; but one day as his governor is reading him a letter about some cuffs his own Miss Luci is crocheting for him, he quietly rips up the ones he is wearing and throws them in the fire.

[6]Aside from the presence of a famous medical school, the air of this seaside city was held to be beneficial and attracted the sick and infirm from Switzerland, England, and elsewhere.

profited me was to provoke envy. Inquisitive and critical attentiveness attached to my every action, and attracted the censure of other women. I did not love those who loved me; I refused a rich man who had neither birth nor breeding; I refused a lord who was shopworn and in debt; I refused a young man whose self-importance was matched only by his stupidity. I was called haughty; my former friends mocked me: the world became hateful to me: my aunt, without reproaching me, pointed out several times that the three thousand pounds which were paid to her annually would cease with her death, and that she had not three thousand in capital to leave me. Such was my situation a year ago, when we went to spend the Christmas holidays with Lady Waltham. I was twenty-five; my heart was sad and empty. I began to curse the tastes and talents that had brought me nothing but vain expectations, hesitations that were misinterpreted, pretensions to a happiness that never came true. There were two men in this house. One, age forty, had returned from the Indies with a considerable fortune. Nothing was said to impugn seriously the manner in which he had acquired it, but neither did he have a brilliant reputation for delicacy and altruism; and in the conversations we had about the riches and the rich of that part of the world, he shunned particulars. He was a handsome man; he was noble in manner and expenditure; he liked fine food, the arts and pleasures; I was to his liking and he spoke to my aunt; he offered a considerable dowry, the ownership of a fine house he had just purchased in London, and three hundred guineas a year in pin money. The other eligible man was the second son of the earl of Reading, thirty-five years of age, four years the widower of a woman who had left him a large fortune, and father of a five-year-old girl of angelic beauty. He is himself of the noblest countenance, he is tall and svelt, and has the kindest blue eyes, the finest teeth, the sweetest smile: that, my dear friend, is how he is or seemed to me then. To me everything he said answered to this attractive appearance. He often spoke with me of the life he lived in the country, the pleasure it would be for him to share its lovely isolation with an amiable and sensitive, able-minded and talented companion. He spoke to me of his daughter and of his desire to give her not a governess or a stepmother, but a mother. Ultimately he spoke yet more plainly, and on the eve of our departure he made my aunt the most generous offers for my hand. If not passionate, I was at least quite moved. Back in London, my aunt made inquiries about my two pretenders; she learned nothing disturbing about the first, but she learned the most advantageous things about the second. Reasonable, knowledgeable, judicious, perfectly even-tempered: every voice thus described Mr. Henley. It was clear to me that I must choose, and you can well imagine, my dear friend, that I gave myself little room for hesitation. It was, in a manner of speaking, the baser part of my heart that preferred Oriental riches, London, greater freedom and more splendid fortune; the nobler part disdained all that and dwelt on the sweetness of an altogether reasonable and sublime happiness such as angels must applaud. If a tyrannical father had forced me to marry the nabob,[7] I would perhaps, out of a sense of duty, have obeyed; and blinding myself to where my fortune might have come from in the light of the good use that I would resolve to make of it, "the blessings of Europe's poor," I would have said to myself, "will turn aside the curses of India." In a word, forced to purchase happiness by such base means, I would have been happy without shame and perhaps even with pleasure; but to give myself of my own choice, in exchange for diamonds, pearls, rugs, perfumes, gold-brocaded muslins, dinners, parties—to this I could not resign myself, and I betrothed myself to Mr. Henley. Our nuptials were delightful. Witty, elegant, decent, considerate, affectionate, Mr. Henley charmed everyone; he was the husband of romance, he seemed to me at times even too perfect; my whims, my ill moods, my moments of impatience found his reason and moderation always in their path. For example, I experienced upon my presentation at court joys and worries that he

---

[7]This word of Indian origin, designating a high official, had acquired by the eighteenth century the specific meaning of "European who had made his fortune in the Indies" (*Petit Robert*, 1967).

seemed not to comprehend. I fondly imagined that the company of a man I so admired would make me become like him; and I left for his estate early in the springtime filled with the best intentions and persuaded that I would be the best wife, the tenderest stepmother, the most worthy mistress of a house ever seen. Sometimes I took as my model the most respectable Roman matrons, at others the wives of our former barons under the feudal government; at still others I pictured myself wandering in the countryside, simple as a shepherdess, gentle as her lambs, and gay as the birds I would hear singing. But this, my dear friend, has made a rather long letter; I shall soon take up the pen again.

Second Letter

We arrived at *Hollow Park*; it is an ancient, lovely and stately mansion that Mr. Henley's mother, heiress of the Astley family, bequeathed to him. I found everything in good order. I was moved when I saw white-haired servants hasten to greet their kind master and bless their new mistress. The child was brought to me; what caresses did I not lavish on her! In my heart I promised her the most devoted attention, the most tender affection. I spent the rest of the day in a sort of delirium; the next day I bedecked the child in finery I had brought her from London, and presented her to her father, for whom I hoped it would be an agreeable surprise.

10

"Your intentions are lovely," he said, "but that is a taste I would not wish to inculcate in her; I would fear that such pretty shoes would prevent her from running about freely; artificial flowers contrast unpleasantly with the simplicity of the countryside."

"You are quite right, sir," I said, "I was wrong to dress her up this way, and now I know not how to take it from her; I tried to win her affection through childish means and have only set her up for a small disappointment and myself for mortification."

Fortunately the shoes were soon ruined, the locket was lost, the flowers in her hat were caught in the thickets where they remained; and I entertained the child so assiduously that she didn't have a chance to miss them. She could read as well in French as in English; *education of young* I decided to have her learn La Fontaine's fables. One day she recited "The Oak and the Reed" to her father with charming grace. I recited the words to myself ahead of her; my heart was pounding and I was flushed with pride.

"She recites wonderfully," said Mr. Henley; "but does she understand what she is saying? Perhaps it were best to fill her head with truths before stuffing it with fictions: history, geography…"

"You are quite right, sir," I said; "but her governess can teach her as well as I that Paris is on the Seine and Lisbon on the Tagus."

11

"Why be so impatient?" Mr. Henley replied gently, "Teach her La Fontaine's fables if that amuses you; in the end little harm will come of it."[8]

"No," I blurted out, "she's not my child, she's yours."

"But my dear, I was hoping..."

I did not respond and departed in tears. I know I was wrong; it was I who was in the wrong. A while later I returned, and Mr. Henley seemed not even to remember my impatience. The child fidgeted and yawned at his side but he did not notice. Some days later I tried to initiate a history and geography lesson; it soon wearied both mistress and pupil. Her father considered her too young to learn music, and suspected that such a talent brought with it more pretensions than delights. The little girl, who henceforth spent all her time with me in boring trifles or watched my movements sometimes stupidly and sometimes with curiosity, got on my nerves; I all but banished her from my room. She had grown estranged from her governess. The poor child is certainly less happy and less well behaved than she was before I came. Were it not for the measles she recently had, and that I caught by caring for her day and night, I would not realize that this child is more important to me than a stranger's. As for the servants, I have not given one of them cause for complaint;

---

[8]Echo of Rousseau's rejection of the practice of teaching La Fontaine to children, in book 2 of *Emile*. But Rousseau did not favor the systematic teaching of lessons to the child, as Henley apparently does.

but my elegant chambermaid has caught the fancy of a farmer of these parts, who previously was in love with the daughter of an elderly and excellent housekeeper, foster sister[9] of my husband's mother. Peggy, disconsolate, and her mother, outraged by the insult, left the house despite all we could say. I try as I can to make up for the loss, with the help of my chambermaid, who is of good character, else I would have dismissed her forthwith; the whole household misses the former housekeeper, and I too, as well as her wonderful preserves.

I had brought with me from London a superb white Angora. To Mr. Henley he was not handsomer than any other cat, and he often joked about the way fashion dictates the fate of animals, bringing them excessive admiration or humiliating scorn, like our dresses and hairdos. Yet he petted the Angora, for he is good and denies to no creature endowed with sensitivity a small token of his own. — But it wasn't exactly the story of my Angora that I wanted to tell you. The walls of my room were hung by sections. Dark green velvet separated panels of needlepoint done by Mr. Henley's grandmother. Heavy armchairs that were very hard to move but very good for sleeping, embroidered in the same hand, bordered in the same velvet, were, along with a very firm settee, all my

---

[9]This term, *sœur de lait* in the French, refers to an unrelated person who was nursed by the same woman. This was felt to form a real bond, analogous to that of blood, though, to be sure, less powerful.

room had by way of furniture. My Angora would lie down unimpressed on these old chairs and catch his claws in the old embroidery. Mr. Henley had several times placed him gently on the floor. Six months ago, as he was about to go hunting, he came to bid me good-bye in my room and saw my cat sleeping on a chair.

"Ah!" said Mr. Henley, "what would my grandmother say, what would my mother say, if they were to see..."

"They would doubtless say," I answered impetuously, "that I must use my furniture as it suits me, as indeed they themselves did, and that I should not be a stranger even in my own room; and for as long as I have complained of these heavy chairs and this dark wall hanging, they would have enjoined you to give me other chairs and brighter walls."

"Give! my dearest life!" replied Mr. Henley, "does one give to oneself? Does half of oneself give to the other? Are you not the mistress of the house? This once passed for most beautiful..."

"Aye, once," I replied; "but I live now."

"My first wife," replied Mr. Henley, "liked these furnishings."

"Oh, God," I cried, "would she were still alive!"

"And all this for a cat I haven't even harmed?" said Mr. Henley gently and sadly, resignedly, and he left.

"No," I cried after him, "it's not the cat"; but he was already far away, and a moment later I heard him in the courtyard calmly giving his orders as he mounted his horse. Such composure was the last straw: I was beside myself. I rang. He had told me I was the mistress; I had the armchairs taken to the parlor, the settee to a storage room. I ordered a lackey to take down the portrait of the first Mrs. Henley, which was opposite my bed.

"But Madam!" the lackey said.

"Do as I say, or leave," was my reply.

He assumed and you probably do as well that I was irritated at the portrait: no, in truth, I think not; but it was attached to the wall hanging, and wanting to do away with that, I had to take down the portrait first. The hanging came next; it was held up only by hooks. I had it properly cleaned and rolled up. I had wicker chairs put in my room, and myself arranged a cushion for my Angora; but the poor animal got no benefit from my attentions: frightened by all the hubbub, he had fled into the woods, and was never seen again. Mr. Henley, having returned from the hunt, had the surprise of finding his wife's portrait in the dining room. He came up to my room without a word, and wrote to London for the finest India wallpaper, the most elegant armchairs and brocaded muslin for the curtains. Was I wrong, my dear friend, other than formally? Have old things more merit than new? And do those who are reputed to be reasonable do anything other, most of the time, than gravely maintain their prejudices and tastes against prejudices and tastes more forcefully expressed?

15

The story of the dog isn't worth telling: I had to make him leave the dining room so often during meals that he doesn't come back there any more, and eats in the kitchen. The question of relatives is more serious. There are some I receive as best I can, because they are not well off; but I yawn in their company, and I never go see them on my own because they are the most tedious people on earth. When Mr. Henley says to me offhand: "Let's go see my cousin so-and-so," I go: I follow in the carriage or on horseback with him; it can hardly be unpleasant. But if he chances to say: "My cousin is a good woman," I say no; she is fault-finding, envious, persnickety. If he says that such and such a cousin is a fine man whom he esteems, I answer that he is a vulgar drunkard: what I say is true; but I am wrong, for it hurts him. I get along fine with my father-in-law; he is middling clever and remarkably good-natured. I embroider his jackets and play the harpsichord for him; but Lady Sara Melvil, my sister-in-law, who spends the summer with him, treats me with such unbearable arrogance that I go rarely to the manor. If Mr. Henley said to me: "For my sake put up with her arrogance, I will love you the more for it: I feel it as much as you do; but I love my father and love my brother: your coldness will gradually estrange them from me, and you yourself will be sorry at the loss of happiness, of tender and natural feelings that you will have occasioned," I would say, infallibly say: "You are quite right, Mr. Henley,

16

I can already feel, I have often felt the regret that you fore-tell; it can only increase, it distresses me and will distress me more than I can say; come now, my dear lord, one affectionate glance from you will give me more pleasure than all the hurt that Lady Sara's ridiculous scorn can inflict." But rather than that, Mr. Henley has observed nothing, can remember nothing... "Now that you men-tion it, my dear, I think I dimly recall... but even so, what of it! How can a reasonable person be affected... and besides, isn't Lady Sara excusable? Daughter of a duke, wife of the future head of our family..." My dear friend, his fists would hurt me less than all this reasoning. I am unhappy and I am bored; I have not brought happiness, nor have I found it here; I have caused disorder, and have not bettered myself; I deplore my every mistake, but no means is given me to do better; I am alone, there is no one to share my feelings with me; I am all the more unhappy because there is nothing to blame, no change to request, nothing to reproach, and that I accuse and despise myself for being unhappy. Everyone admires Mr. Henley and congratulates me on my happiness; I reply: "It is true, you are quite right... What a difference from others of his station, of his age! What a difference between my fate and that of Mrs. this or Lady that." That's what I say, and I think it, but my heart does not feel it; it swells or con-tracts, and often I withdraw to let my tears flow freely. At this very moment tears that I can scarcely explain mix

unhappiness

with the ink on this paper. Farewell, my dear friend, I will write you again very soon.

P.S. Rereading this letter, I have found that I was more in the wrong than I had thought. I shall have the first Mrs. Henley's portrait put back in its former place. If Mr. Henley likes it better in the dining room, where it is in truth in better light, he can return it there; I am going to call the same lackey who took it away. Once he has put the portrait back, I will tell him to have the horses harnessed to the carriage, and shall go see my father-in-law. I shall simply have to say to myself, on behalf of Mr. Henley, the things I wish he had said to me, and I shall put up with Lady Sara Melvil.

Third Letter

You are quite right, my dear friend, it wasn't for me to complain of the injustices that might be occasioned by *The Sentimental Husband*. Yet it was in good faith, and still today my ideas about all that are not too clear. Whether out of patience or indifference, virtue or disposition, it seems to me that Mr. Henley had not believed himself unhappy. He had, I have no doubt, been aware of my every mistake; but as he had never indicated any resentment toward me, or taken measures to avoid renewed mistakes on my part by adopting a conduct that would have tied my soul more closely to his and my pleasures to his, it appeared to me that he had drawn no conclusion from all that. He lived and judged me, so to speak, one day at a time, until the day Mr. and Mrs. Bompré came to render him rather more satisfied with himself and more dissatisfied with me. I have had much cause for sorrow since my last letter. One day when I was deploring my limited ability for household management, my slow improvement, and the ups and downs in my zeal and efforts on this point, Mr. Henley, albeit very openly and with a smile, enumerated all the things that have gone less well since Mistress Grace departed.

"Let us try to win her back," I answered on the spot; "I have heard it said that Peggy was employed in London, and that her mother was getting along poorly with the cousin she went to live with."

"You may try," said Mr. Henley, "I fear you will not succeed; but there is no harm in trying."

"Will you speak to her?" I said to him. "The sight of her former master and the exceptional nature of your overture will help her forget her resentment."

"I can't do it," he replied, "I have business to attend to; but, if you wish, I shall send someone."

"No, I shall go myself."

I called for the carriage, and I went; it is four miles from here. Mistress Grace was alone: she was very surprised to see me. Through the coolness her greeting was meant to convey, I could see that she was moved and embarrassed for reasons I could not divine. I told her how much we had all lost with her departure, how we needed her, how we missed her.

"Do you wish to come back?" I said. "You will be greeted with open arms, you will be respected and cherished. Why hold against us all the inconstancy of a young man who doesn't deserve Peggy's regrets, since he was capable of jilting her; perhaps she has herself forgotten: I have heard that she is employed in London…"

"Employed!" exclaimed Mistress Grace, clasping her hands and lifting her eyes toward heaven. "Have you come here to insult me, Madam?"

"God forbid," I exclaimed in turn, "I have no idea what you mean."

"Ah, Madam!" she said after a long silence, "wounds do not heal as quickly as they are inflicted, and your Fanny, with her lace and ribbons and city airs, has brought my Peggy and her poor mother sufferings that will end only with our lives."

She was weeping bitterly. Encouraged by my kind words and urgings, she told me, sobbing, the story of her woes. Peggy, heartbroken by her lover's departure, and bored with her mother and cousin, left without a word: for a long time they searched for her, and believed she had drowned; finally they learned that she was in London, where her appealing youthfulness won her a place in a house of ill repute. You can imagine what the mother would have added to this sad narrative, all that I would have said, all that I must have felt. Finally I repeated my first proposition. Despite many normal and just protestations whose force I quite understood, I engaged this poor woman to return with me to *Hollow Park*.

"No one," I told her, "will mention your daughter; you will not see Fanny unless you inform me that you so wish: come, my good Mistress Grace, come enjoy our consolations, and end your days in a house where you served well in your youth, and from which I should never have let you go."

I put her in the carriage, not wanting to run the risk that preparing her baggage would give rise to new reflections that would make her hesitate to come. En route she never ceased crying, and I too wept. A hundred yards from the house I got out, and told the driver not to pull up in front until I so ordered. I entered the house alone; I spoke to Mr. Henley, to the child and to Fanny, and to the other servants. Finally I went to fetch Mistress Grace, and giving her my keys, entreated her immediately to take up her functions. Five or six days went by, Fanny obeying scrupulously: she ate and worked in her own room. One day when I had gone to look at her needlework, Mistress Grace came too, and after thanking me for my kindness, she begged me to allow Fanny henceforth to eat with the others and live in the house as before. Fanny was touched, and wept for Peggy and her mother. Poor Fanny! Her turn was to come. Mr. Henley sent for me to go down, and bring her with me. We found with him, in his study, the father of the young farmer.

"Madam," he said to me, "I have come to beg of Mr. Henley and you letters of recommendation for my son for the Indies; it is a place where you can get rich, they say, in short order; he can take Miss Fanny with him, or come back to marry her once he is a rich man. They can do as they see fit; as for me, I will never receive in my house an idle and coquettish city doll, not to mention that I would fear calling down on me a curse from heaven if I brought into my family a girl who by her wretched ways had caused my son's inconstancy and poor Peggy's ruin. My son will do as he pleases, Miss; but I declare before God that he will renounce father and mother if he ever sees you again."

Fanny, pale as death, made to leave; but her legs buckled under her, and she leaned against the door. I ran over to help her, and saw her back to her room. On the stairway we encountered Mistress Grace.

"Your daughter is avenged," Fanny said.

"Lord, what is it?" cried Mistress Grace.

She followed us: I told her what had transpired; she swore that she had had no part in this thing, nor had she ever again seen either the farmer or his son since first leaving the house. I left them alone; I went and shut myself in my room: there I bitterly lamented the fate of these two girls, and all the pain I had caused; finally I wrote to my aunt that I was sending Fanny back, and begged her to find a good place for her, either as companion to a lady or in a shop; and after ordering the driver to harness up as quickly as possible, I went back to Fanny's room, and had her read my letter. The poor girl burst into tears.

"But what have I done?" she said to me.

"Nothing, my poor child, nothing bad; but we absolutely must separate. I shall pay your wages through the end of the year, I shall add more money and linen than you would now even desire from a mistress you consider unjust. I shall write to your parents to send me your younger sister; but you must come with me at once, and I shall take you to where the coach will pass an hour from now; Mistress Grace and I shall take care of everything you leave behind, and you will get it in two days."

The carriage was ready; I got in with her, and practically without uttering a word we came to the place I had mentioned. I waited for the coach; I commended her to those inside, and returned sadder than I can say. "So that," I said to myself, "is what I came to accomplish here. I have brought about the ruin of a poor, innocent girl; I have made another unhappy; I have brought discord between a father and his son; I have filled a mother's soul with bitterness and shame." Driving through the woods, I wept for my Angora; coming into my room I wept for

Fanny. Mistress Grace has acted as my chambermaid ever since. Her sadness, even though she tries to overcome it, is a continual reproach. Mr. Henley has seemed to me surprised at all this commotion. He does not quite understand why I have so suddenly sent off my chambermaid. To him the farmer has done the right thing in opposing his son's marriage. "These women who are used to the city," he says, "never take root in the country, and are not good here": but he thinks the son could have been made to listen to reason, and that I could well have kept Fanny; that they would even have grown apart while continuing to see each other, whereas now the young man's imagination will try to prolong the illusion of love, and he will perhaps make a point of remaining faithful to his persecuted mistress. Let come what may please God; but I have done what I thought I must, and have spared myself scenes that would have compromised my health and utterly altered my temperament. It has been a fortnight since Fanny left. Lady *** will keep her until she has found a place for her. Her sister arrives tonight. She has been in London only long enough to learn how to do hair, and has since been nearly a year back in her village. She isn't pretty, and I shall see to it that she does not become elegant. Farewell, my dear friend.

P.S. My letter could not go out the other day: I was told while sealing it that it was too late.

Fanny's sister is filthy, clumsy, lazy and impertinent; I cannot keep her. Mr. Henley keeps telling me that I was wrong to dismiss a girl whom I liked, who served me well, and against whom there was no reproach. I should not have taken at face value, he says, what John Turner said when he was carried away; the proof is his ridiculous notion of sending to the Indies a boy who doesn't know how to write. He is astonished that we excitable souls fall prey to each others' outbursts and exaggerations. We ought to know, in his opinion, how much we should discount the things that passion inspires us to imagine and say: I have, he says, mistaken an action that did not come easily for an act of generosity, without reflecting that what was disadvantageous to me was not necessarily advantageous to others. It would have been better not to have brought that girl here with me. He thinks he must have intimated as much at the time; but once she was here, since she wasn't guilty of anything, she should have stayed. Could he be right, my dear friend? Could I be wrong again, always wrong, wrong in everything? No, I cannot believe that; it was natural to keep Fanny when I got married. I did not understand Mr. Henley's intimation.

I did not know that it was difficult to get used to living in the country; after all, I myself was coming to live here. Fanny might have proven appealing to a country man; she might have married him; she is sweet and amiable. I could not know that it would be a grief to his family and a misfortune for him. I was not wrong to send her away: I could be neither her jailor nor her accomplice either in helping her see the young man or in turning him away. It was not for me to assume either their woes or their errors. In time, if she forgets her lover, if he marries or moves away, I can bring her back; I do not intend ever to abandon her.

I think nonetheless that I have been too hasty. I could have waited a day or two, consulted Mr. Henley, consulted her, seen what her courage and what the young man's respect for his father could produce. I have too much obeyed my impetuosity of temperament. I have too much feared the sight of unhappy lovers and humiliated pride. May God protect Fanny from misfortune, and me from remorse.

I shall write again to my aunt, and again commend Fanny to her.

Fourth Letter

I go on, my dear friend, about rather uninteresting things, and at what length, in what detail! — But that's the way they are in my head; and I would think I was telling you nothing if I withheld anything. It's little things that disturb and exasperate me, and put me in the wrong. Listen once more to a lot of little things.

Three weeks ago there was a ball in Guilford. Mr. Henley was one of the subscribers. One of his relatives, who has a house there, invited us to come visit her the day before, and to bring the child. We went; I took the clothes I intended to wear, a dress I had worn to a ball in London eighteen months earlier; a hat, feathers and flowers that my aunt and Fanny had chosen expressly for this occasion, and that I had received two days earlier. I had seen them only at the time I put them on, not having yet opened the package. I was quite content; I thought myself very handsome when I was dressed, and I put on some rouge as nearly all women do. An hour before the ball, Mr. Henley arrived from *Hollow Park*.

"You look very fine, Madam," he said, "for you could hardly look otherwise; but to me you are a hundred times more handsome in your most simple apparel than in all this finery. It seems to me, moreover, that a woman of twenty-six shouldn't be dressed like a girl of fifteen, nor a respectable woman like an actress…"

Tears came to my eyes. "Lady Alesford," I replied, "did not think when she sent me all this that she was outfitting a girl of fifteen, or an actress; but her niece, your wife, whose age she knows… But sir, say that this outfit annoys or displeases you, that it would give you pleasure not to see me go out dressed in this fashion, and I shall at once renounce the ball, and, I hope, with good grace."

"Could we not," he said to me, "send a man on horseback to fetch another dress, another hat?"

"No," I said, "it can't be done; I have my chambermaid here, and they wouldn't find anything suitable; I would irreparably dishevel my hair."

"Oh! what difference does it make?" said Mr. Henley, half-smiling.

27

"It makes a difference to me," I cried vehemently; "but you have only to say that I need not go, that I would oblige you, and I shall be happy to oblige." — And half out of spite, half from sentiment, I started to cry in earnest.

"I am very sorry, Madam," said Mr. Henley, "that this affects you so strongly. I shall not prevent you from going to the ball. You have not yet found in me a decidedly despotic husband. My wish is that reason and decency be your rule, and not that you yield to my biases; since your aunt found this outfit suitable, you should remain as you are… now put back on the rouge that your tears have washed out." — I smiled, and kissed his hand in joyful enthusiasm.

"I perceive with pleasure," he said, "that my wife is as youthful as her headdress and as light as her feathers." — I went to put on some more rouge. Some people arrived, and when the time for the ball came, we set out. In the carriage I affected gaiety, in order to inspire some in Mr. Henley and in myself. — I did not succeed. — I didn't know whether I had done well or not. I wasn't happy with myself, and was ill at ease.

We had been in the ballroom for a quarter of an hour; all eyes turned towards the door, drawn by the most noble figure, the simplest, most elegant and magnificent costume. People inquired, whispered, and everyone said: "Lady Bridgewater, the wife of Governor Bridgewater, who has just returned from the Indies and been made a baronet." — Excuse my weakness; this moment was not kind for your friend. Fortunately another object of comparison presented itself: my sister-in-law entered with a hint of rouge; her feathers well outdid mine!

"You see!" said I to Mr. Henley.

"She is not my wife," he replied.

He went to take her hand and escort her to her chair. Others, I thought, will have the same indulgence for me! A bit of coquetry was kindled in my heart, and I shook off my worries the better to be lovable the rest of the night. I had a reason for not dancing, which I won't tell you yet.

After the first quadrille, Lady Bridgewater came and sat beside me.

"I inquired who you were, Madam," she said to me, with utmost graciousness; "and your name alone made me your acquaintance and all but your friend. —It would be too vain of me to admit the part your countenance plays in my predisposition; Sir John Bridgewater, my husband, who has often spoken to me of you, having told me that I look like you."

Such sweetness and candor won me over: all this should have increased my jealousy, and yet I ceased to feel any. It yielded to a gentle sympathy. It may indeed be that Lady Bridgewater looks like me; but she is younger than I: she is taller, more slender: she has handsomer hair: in a word, she has the advantage in every particular about which one cannot delude oneself, and even in the others I can't have any over her, for one cannot possess more grace, or a voice that more speaks to the heart, than she.

Mr. Henley was extremely attentive to Miss Clairville, a most appetizing and gay young lady of the county, yet modest and not at all pretty. For my part, I conversed all night with Lady Bridgewater and with Mr. Mead, her brother, to whom she had introduced me, and all told I was entirely pleased with myself and the others.

I invited them to come visit me: Lady B. expressed her great regret at being obliged to leave the county the very next day to return to London and then rejoin her husband in Yorkshire, where he was standing for election. As for Mr. Mead, he accepted my invitation for the day after next. We parted company as late as we could.

I went and rested for several hours at the house of Mr. Henley's relative, and after lunch my husband, his daughter and I got in the carriage: the governess and my chambermaid had already left. My mind was occupied with Lady B.; and having reviewed in my imagination her pleasant face, and, as it were, again heard her words and expression, "You will agree that she is charming," I said to Mr. Henley.

"Who is that?" he replied.

"Really now," I said, "do you not know?"

"Well you must be talking about Lady B.? Yes, she is very nice, a handsome woman; above all I found that she was well dressed. I can't say that she made a very great impression on me."

"Oh!" I continued, "if small blue eyes, red hair and a peasant air make for beauty, then Miss Clairville certainly

has it over Lady B. and all of her sort. To me, the m
agreeable person I saw at the whole ball after Lady B. was
her brother; he reminded me of Mylord Alesford, my first
suitor, and I asked him to come tomorrow to dine with us."

"How fortunate I am not jealous," said Mr. Henley,
half smiling.

"It is fortunate for you," I replied, "not for me; for if
you were jealous, at least I would see you feel something;
I would be flattered; I would think I mattered to you; I
would think you fear to lose me, that you still find me
pleasing; that at least you think I could still please you.
Oh, yes!" I added, piqued both by my own emotion and
by his inalterable composure, "the injustice of a jealous
husband, the excesses of a tyrant, would be less exasper-
ating than the disinterest and dryness of a sage."

*husband
expresses
no
feeling*

"You would have me believe," said Mr. Henley, "in the
taste of Russian women who want to be beaten. But my
dear, control yourself for the child's sake, and let us not
set an example..."

"You are quite right," I cried out. "Excuse me, sir!
excuse me, dear child!..."

I took her on my lap; I kissed her; I wet her face with
my tears. *So many tears!*

"I am setting a bad example for you," I told her. "I
should be a mother to you; so I had promised, and I have
not looked after you, and I say things in front of you that
you are fortunate enough not to understand fully!"

Mr. Henley said nothing; but I do not doubt that he was moved. The little girl remained on my lap, and gave me caresses that I returned a hundredfold, but in a manner rather more sad than tender. I was bitterly regretful; I thought up all sorts of projects; I promised myself I would finally become a mother to her: but I could see in her eyes, that is to say in her soul, that this was impossible. She is fair, she is not at all ill-natured, she is not devious; but she is hardly excitable or sensitive. — She shall be my pupil, but she will not be my child; she has no desire to be.

We arrived. At my behest the Henley household was invited for the next day. Miss Clairville, who was there, also came. At the table I placed Mr. Mead between her and Lady Sara Melvil, and nothing about the whole day was either unpleasant or remarkable. The next day I wrote a letter to Mr. Henley, and I send you the draft with all its erasures. There are almost as many words crossed out as remaining, and you will not read it without difficulty.

Sir,

I trust you were aware, day before yesterday, of my shame at my extravagant outburst. Do not think that on this occasion or on any other I am insensible to the merit of your patience and gentleness. I can assure you that my intentions have always been good. But what good are intentions when the effect never matches them? — For your part, your conduct is such that I have no accusations to make, however much I sometimes wish I could in order to justify my own. — Yet there is one error you have made; in marrying me you did me too much honor. You believed, as who would not have! that, finding in her husband all that an amiable and estimable man can be, and in her situation every honest pleasure, wealth and consideration, a reasonable woman could not fail to find happiness: but I am not a reasonable woman; you and I have realized this too late. — I do not possess, along with the qualities that you found pleasing, those that would have made you happy. — You could have found both in a thousand other women. You did not ask for brilliant talents, because you settled for me, and assuredly no one is less demanding than you as far as exceptional virtues are concerned. I spoke acrimoniously of Miss Clairville only because I was pained to reflect how much better than I such a girl would have suited you. Accustomed to country pleasures and occupations, active, hard-working, simple in her tastes, grateful, gay, contented, would she have let you remember that there were qualities she lacked? Miss Clairville would have remained here amidst her relatives and familiar surroundings. She would have lost nothing, only gained... But no use dwelling on a mere fantasy... the past cannot be recalled. — Let us talk about the future; above all, let us talk about your daughter. Let us try to arrange my conduct in such a way as to repair my greatest fault. By opposing at the outset my designs for her, you did only what was fair and reasonable; but in so doing, you seemed to find fault with what had been done for me, to disdain all that I knew and was. — I was humiliated and discouraged; I was neither compliant nor really cooperative. In the future I wish to

self deprecation [handwritten annotation]

33

desperate
to please

do my duty; not according to my fancy, but according to your
judgment. I do not ask you to map out a plan for me; I shall try
to divine your thoughts and submit to them: but if I guess wrong
or go about it wrong, do me the favor not simply to censure me,
but to tell me what it is that you wish me to do instead. On this
point as on all others, I sincerely desire to deserve your approval,
to regain or rather gain your affection, and to diminish in your
heart your regret at having made an unfortunate choice.

S. Henley

I took my letter to Mr. Henley in his study, and with-
drew. — A quarter of an hour later, he came to join me in
the parlor.

"Have I complained, madam," he said, embracing me,
"have I talked about Miss Clairville, have I thought of any
Miss Clairville?"

At that moment his father and brother entered, and
I hid my emotion. It seemed to me that during their
visit Mr. Henley was more attentive, and observed me
more often than he did ordinarily; that was the best way
of answering me. We have not spoken of the matter further. Since that day I arise earlier; I have Miss Henley
breakfast with me. She comes to my room for a writing
lesson; I teach her geography also, some elements of
history, some idea of religion. — Ah! if I could learn
it by teaching it, if I could only persuade myself of it
and let it fill my heart! How many flaws would dis-
appear! How many vanities would evaporate in the face

of those truths sublime in their object and eternal in their usefulness!

I will not tell you of my success with the child. We have to wait and hope. Neither will I tell you all the things I do to make the country interesting to me. This place is like its master, everything is too perfect; there is nothing to change, nothing that requires my participation or attention. An old lime tree screens a rather charming view from one of my windows. I wanted to have it felled; but when I looked closely, I myself could see that that would be a pity. The best I can find to do, in this verdant season, is to watch the leaves appear and unfold, the flowers blossom, a cloud of insects fly, creep, run every which way. I don't understand any of it, I apprehend it but superficially; but I contemplate and admire this world that is so full, so alive. I lose myself in this vast whole that is so wonderful, I do not say so wise, for I am too ignorant: I know not its ends, I know neither its means nor its purpose, I do not know why the voracious spider is entitled to so many gnats; but I watch, and hours pass during which I have not thought even once about myself or my childish sufferings.

Fifth Letter

I can no longer doubt it, my dear friend, I am with child; I have just now written to my aunt, and asked her to tell Mr. Henley, who has been in London for several days. I am overjoyed; I shall redouble my attentions to Miss Henley. For more than a year I was nothing to her; the

last two months I have been a tolerable mother, I must
not become a stepmother. Farewell. You shall have no
more news today.

Sixth Letter

I am not too well, my dear friend. I cannot tell you all at
once what is on my mind to say. The task is long and
hardly pleasant. I shall rest when I get tired. — It matters
little whether you receive my letter a few weeks sooner
or later. After this one, I do not wish to write any more in
this style. A note will inform you from time to time that
your friend still lives until she no longer does.

My situation is sad, or else I am a being without reason
or virtue. — Given this vexing alternative of blaming fate,
which I cannot alter, or blaming and despising myself,
whichever way I turn, the pictures that come to my mind,
the details that so crowd my memory, undermine my
courage and render my existence gloomy and painful.
—What good does it do to relive in the telling the painful
images and retrace scenes that cannot be too soon or too
completely forgotten? For the last time you shall see into
my heart; after that I will allow myself no more com-
plaining: it must change or evermore remain closed.

When I thought my pregnancy was certain, I had my
aunt so inform Mr. Henley. He returned from London
only a week later. In the meantime I had been continually
asking myself whether I ought or wanted to nurse my
child. — On the one hand, I was frightened to think how

tiring it would be, what continual attention and privations it would entail. — Shall I say it? I was also frightened by the injury wrought on a woman's figure by the nurse's function. On the other hand, I feared as a great humiliation the idea of being thought unable and unworthy of fulfilling this duty. But, you will say, have you then only pride? Did you not imagine an extreme pleasure in being all for your child, attaching it to you, attaching yourself to it by every available bond? Yes, to be sure, and that was indeed my most constant preoccupation; but when one is alone, and thinking always on the same thing, what does one not think?

I resolved to discuss this with Mr. Henley; and it was not without difficulty that I broached the matter. I was equally apprehensive lest he approve my design as something necessary, that went without saying, that it was awful even to put in doubt; and lest he reject it as something absurd and for reasons that would humiliate me.

I was spared neither of these mortifications. — In his opinion, nothing on earth could exempt a mother from her first and most sacred duty, save the danger of harming her child through some vice of temperament or fault of character,[10] and he told me that his intention was to

---

[10]In the medical theory of the time, aspects of temperament, which is based on the interplay of bodily humors (fluids), might well be communicable through breast feeding. This discussion calls attention to the great popular emphasis on maternal nursing in the wake of Rousseau's argument for it in *Emile* (1762).

consult his friend Dr. M., to learn whether my extreme nervousness and frequent impatience indicated that a stranger would be preferable. Of me, my health, my pleasure, not a word: the only concern was this child that did not yet exist. — This time I did not protest, did not get carried away, I was only saddened; but so profoundly that my health was affected. Why, I said to myself, not one of my thoughts will be divined, none of my feelings shared, no suffering will be spared me! Everything I feel is then absurd, or else Mr. Henley is insensible and hard. I shall spend my entire life with a husband in whom I inspire only perfect indifference, and whose heart is closed to me. Farewell the joy of motherhood; farewell every joy. I fell into utter dejection. Mistress Grace was the first to notice, and spoke about it to Mr. Henley, who could not conceive the cause. He thought that my condition made me apprehensive, and suggested that I have my aunt come visit me. I gratefully endorsed this idea. We wrote, and my aunt came. — Tomorrow, if I can, I shall take up the pen again.

I said nothing of this to my aunt, and less sought consolation in her tenderness than diversion in her conversation. Anything emotional plunged me back into thoughts of my sorrows: to escape them, I needed to escape from myself, distract and forget myself, forget my whole situation.

The intrigues of court, news of the city, liaisons, marriages, appointments, all the vanities and all the frivolities of high society restored my own frivolity and a sort of gaiety: what a perilous gift! Its benefit was only passing, and only led to new sorrows.

Soon I thought of my son or daughter only as a prodigy of beauty, whose brilliant talents, cultivated by the most stunning education, would excite the admiration of the whole surrounding country, nay all of Europe. — My daughter, lovelier yet than Lady Bridgewater, chose a husband among the noblest in the kingdom. My son, were he to take up arms, became a hero and commanded armies: if he gave himself to law, he would be at least Lord Mansfield or chancellor; but a permanent chancellor whom the king and people could no longer do without... My head filled with such extravagance, I could hardly avoid letting Mr. Henley notice something of it. Still I laughed at my folly; for I was not completely mad. — One day, half in jest and half reasoning or trying to, I unfurled my fantasies... But I have become so agitated in relating them that I shall have to put down the pen.

We were alone, Mr. Henley said to me: "Our ideas are very different; my wish is that my daughters be brought up in great simplicity; that they not attract attention, and think little of doing so; that they be modest, kind, reasonable, obliging women and vigilant mothers; that they know how to enjoy riches, but above all know how to do without; that their position serve more to sustain virtue than to make their lives easy: and if one cannot have all these things," he said, kissing my hand, "I shall be content with half of the grace, charms and polish of Mistress Henley. — As for my son, a robust body, a healthy mind; that is, exempt from vice and weakness, the strictest probity, which supposes extreme moderation; that is what I ask of God for him. But, my dear friend," he said, "since you attach such importance to all that is brilliant, I would not have you run the risk of learning from someone else something that happened a few days ago. Your first reaction might be to be too affected by it, and so betray to the public, through some sign of trouble, that husband and wife are not of one heart and mind, nor share the same way of thinking and feeling. I have been offered a seat in Parliament, and an appointment at court: I was given to understand I might obtain a title, and an appointment for you; but I refused."

"Nothing could seem more natural, sir," I replied, leaning my face on my hand for fear that my emotion would show, and I spoke slowly in a voice as natural as I could make it, "nothing could seem more natural, if someone had hoped by such offers to purchase a vote contrary to your principles; but you approve the policies of the present ministry?"

"I do," he answered, "I am attached to the king, and I approve today what the ministers are doing. But am I sure I will approve what they will do tomorrow? Is it certain that these ministers will retain their posts? And would I run the risk of seeing a cabal, my peers, take away from me an office that has nothing to do with a political system? Forced then to return to this place that I have always cherished, isn't there the risk that it would be spoiled, changed for me because I would myself be changed, and would bring back with me my wounded pride, frustrated ambition, passions that until now are unknown to me?"

"I admire you, sir," I said, and indeed I had never so admired him; the greater the disappointment, the more I admired him, never had I so clearly realized his superiority. "I admire you; yet the public good, the duty of serving one's country…"

"That is the pretext of the ambitious," he interrupted; "but the good that can be done in one's own house, among one's neighbors, friends, relatives, is much more certain and indispensable: if I do less than I should, it is my fault, and not that of my situation. I have lived too long in London and the other large cities of the Continent. When there I lost sight of the occupations and interests of country people. I lack the gift of conversing with them and learning from them, and the energy I wish I had. I would take my shortcomings with me into public office, and would moreover be to blame for having gotten myself there, whereas Providence has placed me here."

"I have nothing more to answer, sir," I said; "but why did you keep this matter secret from me?"

"I was in London," he replied; "it would have been difficult to explain all my reasons in a letter. If you had

41

objected your own reasons and tastes, I wouldn't have been shaken, and it would have been my displeasure to inflict upon you a displeasure that could have been avoided. Even today I have been sorry to tell you about it; and had I not learned that the thing has become virtually public knowledge, you should never have known of either the proposal or the refusal."

A moment passed after Mr. Henley had finished speaking. I wanted to say something; but I had been so attentive, and was so fiercely torn between my esteem for such moderation, reason, and rectitude in my husband, and the horror of finding such sentiments so foreign to me, and myself so excluded from his thoughts, so useless, so isolated, that I could not speak. I was exhausted by so much effort, and my head spun; I fainted. The care lavished on me precluded any serious consequences of the accident; I am not yet quite recovered, however. Neither my soul nor body is in a normal state. I am but a woman, I will not take my own life, I would not have the courage; if I become a mother, I hope I will never desire to do so; but grief too kills. In a year, in two years, you will learn, I trust, that I am reasonable and contented, or that I am no more.